⌐Preface¬

This is my First Printed project
I never expected my first Project to be a
homo erotic parody of a fairy tale..

For a first Project my technical skills were still
developing, and it shows.
Started roughly 2016, experimenting
with longer projects bit by bit, painting...

The idea just seemed natural, the euphemisms
and innuendo of huffing and puffing, devouring
the Three Not so Little Pigs, and Blowing them away.
Yeah this all started out as casual wordplay.

I never expected it to be received well
when I started sketching a story randomly
in a journal. Having gone through two Redraws
and even expanding beyond the original .

I wish I had something more poignant
to say about the whole thing,
But if you're reading this, thank you
for taking a chance on this vanity project

Now on to the "To-Bed Time Story"

Get it? 'To Bed'? bedtime story?
eh, they can't all be winners.

HickeyBickeyboo

Disclaimer:

The story deals with
explicit homosexualsexual relations.
You must be <u>18 years old</u>
or older to read this publication

All characters depicted are
over the age of 18
References to actual characters,
people, places, etc
are purely coincidental

It seems ambiguous but
for Clarity's sake
the Three Pigs are
<u>NOT</u> directly related to each other,
but are close companions

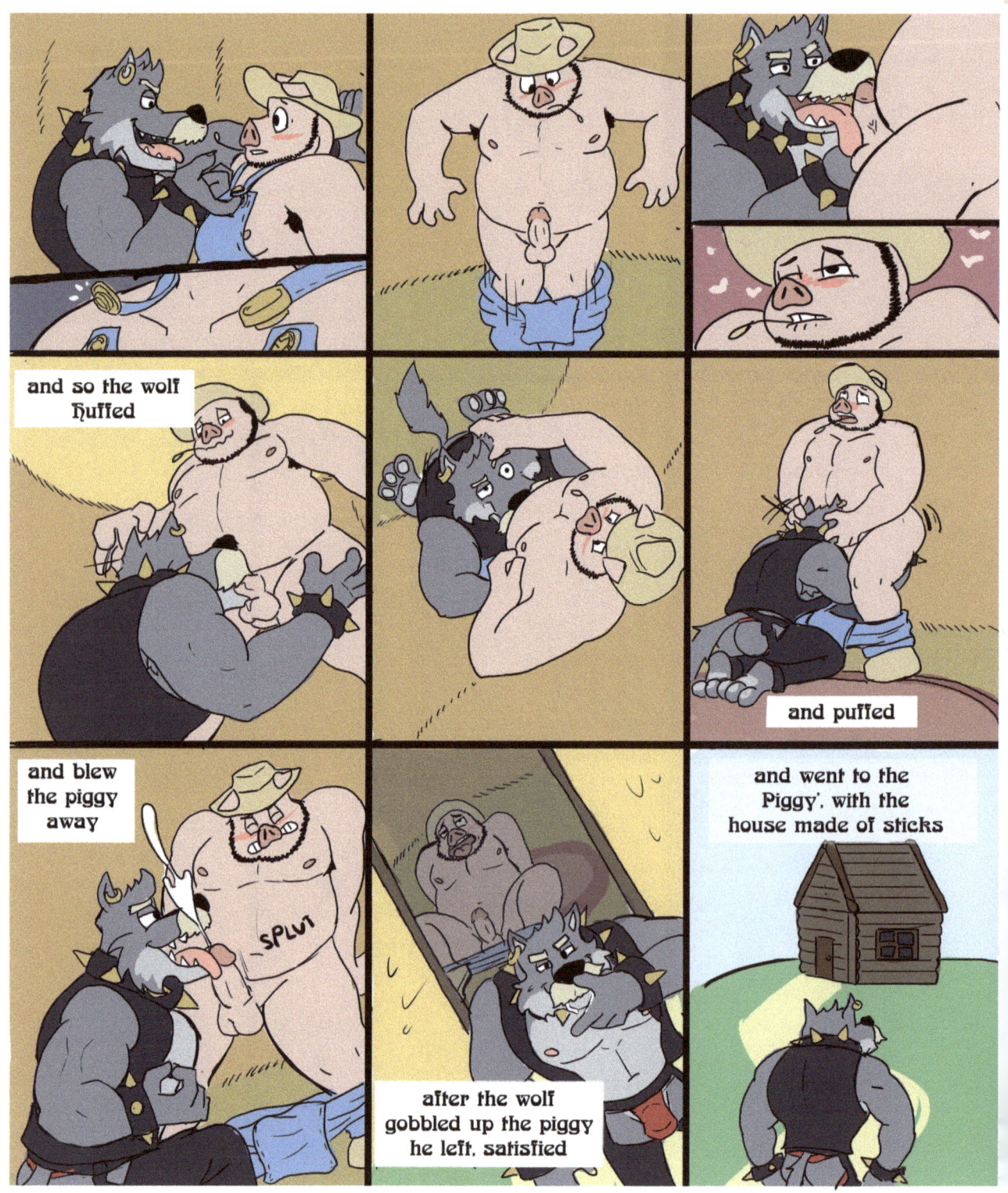

In The End the Straw Piggy, The Wood Piggy
the Brick Piggy, decided to keep
The Big Bad Wolf

and they Lived Happily Ever After

Fin

Lincon was the still the shyest, being the most inexperienced in sex
BB, was more than happy to teachim all he knew about the act
building his confidence.

Logan would periodically invite BB on his Logging ventures in the woods
He'd always somehow bring back less lumber on these days
for some reason

Ever Since BB moved in, Lonny has a renewed Vigor in his life
He loved having BB help him find all the ways this Piggy
could Pop

The Original Page Sketchs

circa 2016

The Original page sketches 1/4

circa 2016

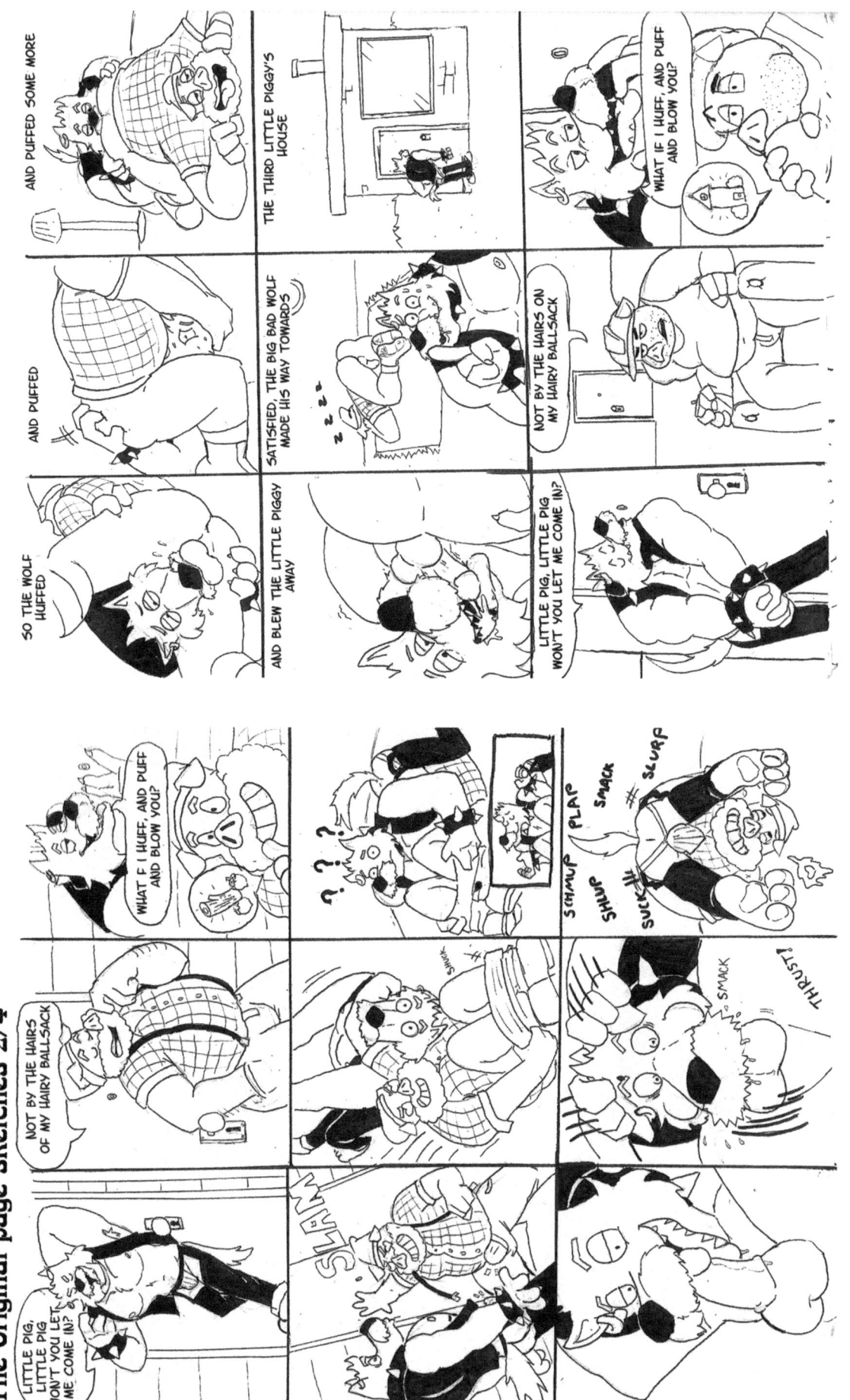

The Original page sketches 2/4

circa 2016

The Original page sketches 3/4

The Original page sketches 4/4

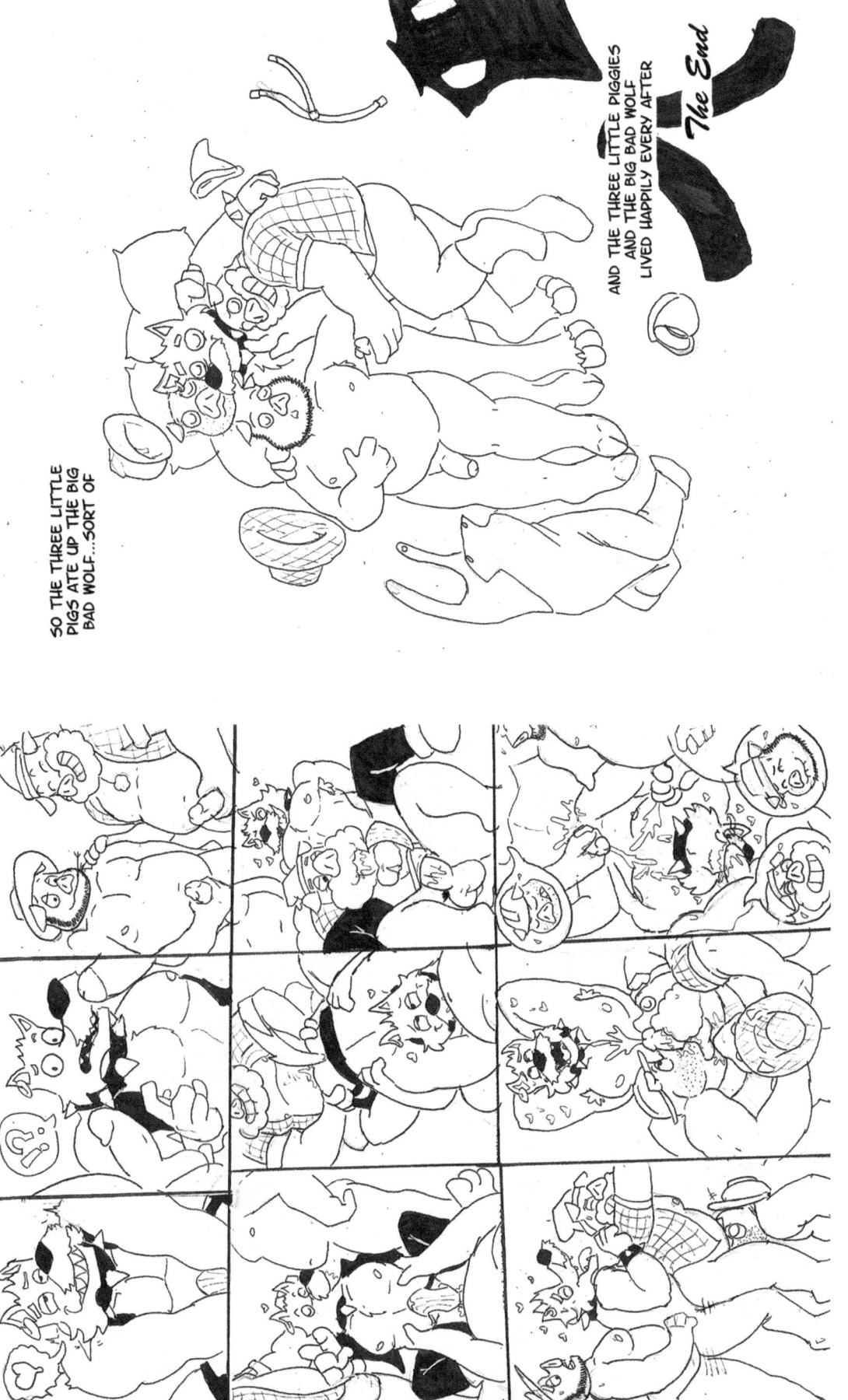

SO THE THREE LITTLE
PIGS ATE UP THE BIG
BAD WOLF...SORT OF

AND THE THREE LITTLE PIGGIES
AND THE BIG BAD WOLF
LIVED HAPPILY EVERY AFTER

The End

circa 2016

Up to now there is no agreed meaning behind the BB
he is nicknamed 'Baby' or Bby by the others